This
Treasure Cove Story
belongs to

**WINNIE THE POOH
THE HONEY TREE**

A CENTUM BOOK 978-1-913265-96-0
Published in Great Britain by Centum Books Ltd.
This edition published 2020.

1 3 5 7 9 10 8 6 4 2

© 2020, 2005, 1958, 1928 Disney Enterprises, Inc.
Illustrations copyright © 2020, 2005, 1968, 1964 Disney Enterprises, Inc.
Based on the *Winnie the Pooh* works by A A Milne and E H Shepard.
All Rights Reserved.

Centum Books Ltd, 20 Devon Square, Newton Abbot,
Devon, TQ12 2HR, UK.

www.centumbooksltd.co.uk | books@centumbooksltd.co.uk
CENTUM BOOKS Limited Reg. No. 07641486.

A CIP catalogue record for this book is available
from the British Library.

Printed in China.

centum

A Treasure Cove Story

Disney
Winnie the Pooh
The Honey Tree

Illustrated by the Walt Disney Studio
Adapted by Bob Totten

Once upon a time, a very long time ago now, about last
Friday, Winnie the Pooh lived in a forest all by himself
under the name of Sanders.

(That means that he had the name over the door
in gold letters, and lived under it.)

One day when he was out walking, he came to an open place in the middle of the forest and in the middle of this place was a large oak tree and, from the top of the tree, there came a loud buzzing noise.

Winnie the Pooh sat down at the foot of the tree, put his head between his paws, and began to think.

First of all he said to himself: 'That buzzing noise means something. You don't get a buzzing noise like that, just buzzing and buzzing, without it meaning something. If there's a buzzing noise, somebody's making a buzzing noise, and the only reason for making a buzzing noise that *I* know of is because you're a bee.'

Then he thought another long time, and said: 'And the only reason for being a bee that I know of is making honey.'

And then he got up, and said: 'And the only reason for making honey is so as *I* can eat it.' So he began to climb the tree.

He
climbed
and he
climbed
and he
climbed,
and as
he climbed
he sang
a little
song
to himself.

It went like this:
'Isn't it funny
How a bear likes honey?
Buzz! Buzz! Buzz!
I wonder why he does?'

Then he climbed a little further... and then just a little
further. By that time he had thought of another song.

    'It's a very funny thought that, if bears were bees,

    They'd build their nests at the *bottom* of trees.

    And that being so (if the bees were bears),

    We shouldn't have to climb up all these stairs.'

    He was getting rather tired by this time, so that is why
he sang a Complaining Song. He was nearly there now,
and if he just stood on that branch... *Crack!*

    'Oh, help!' said Pooh, as he dropped ten feet on to the
branch below him.

    'If only I hadn't—' he said, as he bounced twenty feet
on to the next branch.

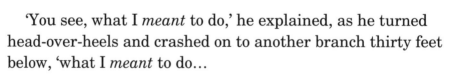

'You see, what I *meant* to do,' he explained, as he turned
head-over-heels and crashed on to another branch thirty feet
below, 'what I *meant* to do...

Of course, it *was* rather...' he admitted, as he slithered very
quickly through the next six branches.

'It all comes, I suppose,' he decided, as he said good-bye to the
last branch, spun round three times, and flew gracefully into
a gorse bush, 'it all comes of *liking* honey so much. Oh, help!'

He crawled out of the gorse bush, brushed
the prickles from his nose, and began to think
again. And the first person he thought of was
Christopher Robin.

So Winnie the Pooh went round to his friend Christopher
Robin, who lived behind a green door in another part
of the forest.

'Good morning, Christopher Robin,' he said.

'Good morning, Winnie the Pooh,' said Christopher Robin.

'I wonder if you've got such a thing as a balloon about you?'

'A balloon?'

'Yes, I just said to myself coming along: "I wonder if
Christopher Robin has such a thing as a balloon about him?"
I just said it to myself, thinking of balloons, and wondering.'

'What do you want a balloon for?' said Christopher Robin.

Winnie the Pooh looked round to see that no one was listening, put his paw to his mouth, and said in a deep whisper: *'Honey!'*

'But you don't get honey with balloons!'

'I do,' said Pooh.

Well, it just happened that Christopher Robin had been to a party the day before at the house of his friend Piglet, and they had balloons at the party. Christopher Robin had had a big green balloon; and one of Rabbit's relations had had a big blue one and had left it behind, being really too young to go to a party at all; and so Christopher Robin had brought the green one *and* the blue one home with him.

'Which one would you like?' he asked Pooh.

Pooh put his head between his paws and thought very carefully.

'It's like this,' he said. 'When you go after honey with a balloon, the great thing is not to let the bees know you're coming. Now, if you have a green balloon, they might think you were only part of the tree, and not notice you, and if you have a blue balloon, they might think you were only part of the sky, and not notice you, and the question is: Which is most likely?'

'Wouldn't they notice *you* underneath the balloon?' asked Christopher Robin.

'They might or they might not,' said Winnie the Pooh. 'You never can tell with bees.' He thought for a moment and said:

'I shall try to look like a small black cloud. That will deceive them.'

'Then you had better have the blue balloon,' said Christopher Robin; and so it was decided.

Well, they both went out with the blue balloon and Christopher Robin took his toy gun with him, just in case, as he always did, and Winnie the Pooh went to a very muddy place that he knew of, and rolled and rolled until he was black all over; and then, when the balloon was blown up as big as big, and Christopher Robin and Pooh were both holding on to the string, Christopher Robin let go suddenly and Pooh Bear floated gracefully up into the sky, and stayed there – level with the top of the tree and about twenty feet away from it.

'Hooray!' shouted Christopher Robin.

'Isn't that fine?' shouted Winnie the Pooh down to him. 'What do I look like?'

'You look like a bear holding on to a balloon,' said Christopher Robin.

'Not,' said Pooh anxiously, ' – not like a small black cloud in a blue sky?'

'Not very much.'

'Ah, well, perhaps from up here it looks different. And, as I say, you never can tell with bees.'

There was no wind to blow him nearer to the tree, so there he stayed. He could see the honey, he could smell the honey, but he couldn't quite reach the honey.

After a little while he called down.

'Christopher Robin!' he said in a loud whisper.

'Hallo!'

'I think the bees *suspect* something!'

'What sort of thing?'

'I don't know. But something tells me they're *suspicious!*'

'Perhaps they think that you're after their honey.'

'It may be that. You never can tell with bees.'

There was another little silence, and then he called down
again, 'Christopher Robin!'

'Yes?'

'Have you an umbrella in your house?'

'I think so.'

'I wish you would bring it out here, and walk up and down
with it, and look up at me every now and then, and say
"Tut-tut, it looks like rain." I think, if you did that, it would
help the deception which we are practising on these bees.'

Well, Christopher Robin laughed to himself, 'Silly old Bear!'
but he didn't say it aloud because he was so fond of Pooh, and
he went home for his umbrella.

'Oh, there you are!' called down Winnie the Pooh, as soon as Christopher Robin got back to the tree. 'I was beginning to get anxious. I have discovered that the bees are now definitely suspicious.'

'Shall I put my umbrella up?' said Christopher Robin.

'Yes, but wait a moment. We must be practical. The important bee to deceive is the Queen Bee. Can you see which is the Queen Bee from down there?'

'No.'

'A pity. Well, now, if you walk up and down with your umbrella, saying, "Tut-tut, it looks like rain," I shall do what I can by singing a little Cloud Song, such as a cloud might sing… Go!'

So, while Christopher Robin walked up and down and wondered if it would rain, Winnie the Pooh sang this song:

'How sweet to be a Cloud
Floating in the Blue!
Every little cloud
Always sings aloud.

How sweet to be a Cloud
Floating in the Blue!
It makes him very proud
To be a little cloud.'

The bees were still buzzing as suspiciously as ever. Some of them, indeed, left their nest and flew all round the cloud as it began the second verse of this song, and one bee sat down on the nose of the cloud for a moment, and then got up again.

'Christopher – *ow!* – Robin,' called out the cloud.

'Yes?'

'I have just been thinking, and I have come to a very important decision. *These are the wrong sort of bees.*'

'Are they?'

'Quite the wrong sort. So I should think they would make the wrong sort of honey, shouldn't you?'

'Would they?'

'Yes. So I think I shall come down.'

'How?' asked Christopher Robin.

Winnie the Pooh hadn't thought about this. If he let go of the string, he would fall – *bump* – and he didn't like the idea of that. So he thought for a long time, and then he said:

'Christopher Robin, you must shoot the balloon with your toy gun. Have you got your toy gun?'

'Of course I have,' said Christopher Robin. 'But if I do that, it will spoil the balloon.'

'But if you *don't,*' said Pooh, 'I shall have to let go, and that would spoil me.'

When he put it like this, Christopher Robin saw how it was and he aimed very carefully at the balloon and fired.

'*Ow!*' said Pooh.

'Did I miss?' asked Christopher Robin.

'You didn't exactly *miss,*' said Pooh, 'but you missed the *balloon.*'

'I'm so sorry,' said Christopher Robin and he fired again, and this time he hit the balloon and the air came slowly out, and Winnie the Pooh floated down to the ground.

But his arms were so stiff from holding on to the string of the balloon all that time that they stayed up straight in the air for more than a week, and whenever a fly came and settled on his nose he had to blow it off. And I think, but I am not sure, that *that* is why he was always called Pooh.

Treasure Cove Stories

Please contact Centum Books
to receive the full list of titles in
the *Treasure Cove Stories* series.
books@centumbooksltd.co.uk

Classic favourites

1 Three Little Pigs
2 Snow White and
the Seven Dwarfs
3 The Fox and the Hound
- Hide-and-Seek
4 Dumbo
5 Cinderella
6 Cinderella's Friends
7 Alice in Wonderland
8 Mad Hatter's Tea Party
from Alice in Wonderland
9 Mickey Mouse and
his Spaceship
10 Peter Pan
11 Pinocchio
12 Mickey and the Beanstalk
13 Sleeping Beauty
and the Good Fairies
14 The Lucky Puppy
15 Chicken Little
16 The Incredibles
17 Coco
18 Winnie the Pooh and Tigger
19 The Sword in the Stone
20 Mary Poppins
21 The Jungle Book
22 The Aristocats
23 Lady and the Tramp
24 Bambi
25 Bambi - Friends of the Forest

Recently published

50 Frozen
51 Cinderella is my Babysitter
52 Beauty and the Beast
- I am the Beast
53 Blaze and the Monster Machines
- Mighty Monster Machines
54 Blaze and the Monster Machines
- Dino Parade!
55 Teenage Mutant Ninja Turtles
- Follow the Ninja!

56 I am a Princess
57 The Big Book of Paw Patrol
58 Paw Patrol
- Adventures with Grandpa!
59 Paw Patrol - Pirate Pups!
60 Trolls
61 Trolls Holiday
62 The Secret Life of Pets
63 Zootropolis
64 Ariel is my Babysitter
65 Tiana is my Babysitter
66 Belle is my Babysitter
67 Paw Patrol
- Itty-Bitty Kitty Rescue
68 Moana
69 Nella the Princess Knight
- My Heart is Bright!
70 Guardians of the Galaxy
71 Captain America
- High-Stakes Heist!
72 Ant-Man
73 The Mighty Avengers
74 The Mighty Avengers
- Lights Out!
75 The Incredible Hulk
76 Shimmer & Shine
- Wish Upon a Sleepover
77 Shimmer & Shine - Backyard Ballet
78 Paw Patrol - All-Star Pups!
79 Teenage Mutant Ninja Turtles
- Really Spaced Out!
80 I am Ariel
81 Madagascar
82 Jasmine is my Babysitter
83 How to Train your Dragon
84 Shrek
85 Puss in Boots
86 Kung Fu Panda
87 Beauty and the Beast - I am Belle
88 The Lion Guard
- The Imaginary Okapi
89 Thor - Thunder Strike!
90 Guardians of the Galaxy
- Rocket to the Rescue!
91 Nella the Princess Knight
- Nella and the Dragon
92 Shimmer & Shine
- Treasure Twins!

93 Olaf's Frozen Adventure
94 Black Panther
95 Trolls
- Branch's Bunker Birthday
96 Trolls - Poppy's Party
97 The Ugly Duckling
98 Cars - Look Out for Mater!
99 101 Dalmatians
100 The Sorcerer's Apprentice
101 Tangled
102 Avengers
- The Threat of Thanos
103 Puppy Dog Pals
- Don't Rain on my Pug-Rade
104 Jurassic Park
105 The Mighty Thor
106 Doctor Strange

Latest publications

107 Captain Marvel
108 The Invincible Iron Man
109 Black Panther
- Warriors of Wakanda
110 The Big Freeze
111 Ratatouille
112 Aladdin
113 Aladdin - I am the Genie
114 Seven Dwarfs Find a House
115 Toy Story
116 Toy Story 4
117 Paw Patrol - Jurassic Bark!
118 Paw Patrol
- Mighty Pup Power!
119 Shimmer & Shine
- Pet Talent Show!
120 SpongeBob SquarePants
- Krabby Patty Caper
121 The Lion King - I am Simba
122 Winnie the Pooh
- The Honey Tree
123 Frozen II
124 Baby Shark and the
Colours of the Ocean
125 Baby Shark and
the Police Sharks!
126 Trolls World Tour

Book list may be subject to change.